A Christmas gift

for

....

"... the greatest gift of all is doing that
little something extra for someone."

SCHULZ

PUFFIN BOOKS

Published by the Penguin Group: London, New York,
Australia, Canada, India, Ireland, New Zealand and South Africa

Penguin Books Ltd, Registered Offices: 80 Strand, London WC2R 0RL, England

puffinbooks.com

First published 2014
001

Peanuts created by Charles M. Schulz
Text by Lauren Holowaty
Line illustrations by Tom Brannon

Copyright © Peanuts Worldwide LLC 2014
Peanuts.com

British Library Cataloguing in Publication Data
A CIP catalogue record for this book is available from the British Library

ISBN: 978–0–723–29406–1

Printed and bound in Portugal

Merry Christmas Snoopy!

By **Charles M. Schulz**

PUFFIN

It was Christmas-time. Snow covered the ground, festive music filled the air and everyone dashed about full of joy . . .

Snoopy was **especially** cheerful. His doghouse was covered with lights and he hummed a tune as he finished his Christmas preparations.

Charlie Brown **had** been cheerful. But his tree did not look quite as good as he had hoped.

. . . CHRISTMAS IS FOR **SHARING**!

THIS IS GOING TO BE A **BAD** CHRISTMAS.

And then PHUT!
The lights on the tree went out.
Now it looked even **worse**.

"Year after year I end up with the **WORST** Christmas tree," sighed Charlie Brown.

"Forget about the past," said his sister, Sally.

"And think about buying my **PRESENT!**"

Charlie Brown emptied his money box . . .

"A piece of string, two sticky sweets, some dog hair, a button and a five-cent coin! That should be enough."

. . . and set off for the shopping mall with his Christmas list.

It was **not** a successful trip.
"I hate present shopping," he groaned. "I couldn't find anything, and it's almost Christmas . . ."

GOOD GRIEF!

Charlie Brown decided to ask Lucy for some advice.

"Christmas shopping is driving me nuts!" he complained.
"I can't buy ANY gifts with five cents!"

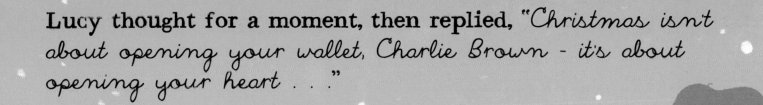

Lucy thought for a moment, then replied, "Christmas isn't about opening your wallet, Charlie Brown - it's about opening your heart . . ."

PSYCHIATRIC HELP 5¢

...FIVE CENTS, PLEASE!

SIGH

THE DOCTOR IS IN

Charlie Brown trudged home. He had **NO** presents and now he had **NO** money.

"*Open my heart, open my heart,*" he said, kicking through the snow. "*What does that mean?*"

Looking up, he saw Snoopy giving Woodstock a gift he had made.

"I know!" thought Charlie Brown. "I'll **MAKE** everyone gifts."

UH-OH . . .

Charlie Brown set to work.

Peppermint Patty's gift was a pair of snowshoes. "I thought these would be perfect for you," he said.

MERRY CHRISTMAS!

She strapped them on and trekked along the snowy path.

But the shoes were SO heavy
she slowly sank,
        deeper
                and deeper into the snow.

THANKS FOR THE
SWELL GIFT, CHUCK.

Charlie Brown made some
special ice skates for Lucy.
"*Because your advice is
the* **BEST**," he said.

MERRY
CHRISTMAS!

Lucy tried to glide, but the blades were **very** wobbly so she almost fell over.

Luckily, Snoopy's special triple axel jump sent her sailing off the lake to safety.

YOU STUPID **BEAGLE!**

BUMP!

Charlie Brown gave Linus some skis.
"Thank you, Charlie Brown!"
said Linus, a little doubtfully.

MERRY CHRISTMAS!

Linus slid down the slope, going **faster** and **faster**,
until he hit a bump and flew into the air.

UH-OH!

Charlie Brown had made
a sledge for Sally.

MERRY
CHRISTMAS!

THANKS,
BIG BROTHER!

She went straight outside, leapt on and **raced** down the hill.
"Doesn't this make you feel Christmassy, Snoopy?" said Charlie Brown.

"Christmas lights are all around . . ."

"My presents are all a **DISASTER!**" cried Charlie Brown. "This really is the **WORST** Christmas ever."

"Look on the bright side, Chuck," said Peppermint Patty . . .

"... At least you got everyone **TOGETHER** for Christmas!"

"This is the **BEST** Christmas ever!" cheered Charlie Brown,
finally realizing it's not what's **under** the tree that matters,
it's who's **around** it.

* MERRY CHRISTMAS, SNOOPY! XXX

The End